THE INCAS

Peter Chrisp

Thomson Learning • New York

Look into the Past

The Ancient Chinese
The Ancient Japanese
The Anglo-Saxons
The Aztecs
The Egyptians
The Greeks
The Incas
The Maya
The Normans
The Romans
The Sioux
The Vikings

First published in the
United States in 1994 by
Thomson Learning
115 Fifth Avenue
New York, NY 10003

First published in in Great Britain in 1994 by
Wayland (Publishers) Ltd.

Library of Congress Cataloging-in-Publication Data
Chrisp, Peter.
  The Incas / Peter Chrisp.
       p.   cm.—(Look into the past)
  Includes bibliographical references and index.
  ISBN 1-56847-171-8
  1. Incas—Juvenile literature. 2. Indians of South America
—Andes Region—Juvenile literature. [1. Incas.
2. Indians of South America.] I. Title. II. Series.
F3429.C52   1994
980'.013—dc20   94-4553

Printed Italy

Picture acknowledgments
The publishers wish to thank the following for providing the photographs in this book: Archiv für Kunst und Geschichte, Berlin 7 (both), 9 (both), 12; Bodleian Library, Oxford (Mason. BB. 56. Vol. 6.) 28; E.T. Archive *cover*, 6 (bottom Amano Museum, Lima), 8 (top Brunning Museum, Lima, bottom Archaeological Museum, Lima), 13, 14 (University Museum, Cuzco), 15 (both, right Archaeological Museum, Lima), 16, 17 (top), 21 (bottom), 23 (bottom), 26; Werner Forman Archive *cover*, 22 (Staatliche Museum, Berlin), 27 (top David Bernstein Fine Art, New York, bottom Museum für Volkerkunde, Berlin), 29 (top British Museum); Nick Saunders/ Barbara Heller 24, 25 (top); South American Pictures/ Tony Morrison *cover*, 4, 6 (top), 10, 11 (both), 17 (bottom), 18, 19, 20, 22 (top), 25 (bottom), 29 (bottom); South American Pictures/ Robert Francis 21 (top).
Map artwork by Jenny Hughes.

CONTENTS

Words that appear in **_bold italic_** in the text are explained in the glossary on page 30.

WHO WERE THE INCAS?

The Andes mountain range stretches down the west coast of South America, through the countries of Ecuador, Peru, Bolivia, and Chile. Five hundred years ago, there was an *empire* in those high mountains, ruled by a people we call the Incas. The word Inca means "lord," and it was the title of the rulers of the empire. They spoke a language called Quechua, which was the name the Inca people called themselves. Although the empire no longer exists, there are still six million Quechua speakers in the lands the Incas once ruled.

This is Machu ▶ Picchu, the ruins of an Inca town almost two miles above sea level. Other Inca towns, such as Cuzco, are even higher. No other people in the world built towns as high as the Incas. They were well suited to life in the mountains. The people had large lungs, which helped them to breathe the thin mountain air.

The Inca empire ▶ was built up in less than a hundred years. This was thanks to the **conquests** of three great Inca rulers: Pachacuti, his son Topa Inca, and Topa Inca's son, Huayna Capac. By the time of Huayna Capac's death, around 1525, the Incas ruled over more than twelve million people, speaking at least twenty different languages. Their empire was more than 2,000 miles long, linked up by nearly 30,000 miles of well built roads.

The Incas called their empire "Tahuantisuyu," which means "The Land of the Four Quarters." It was divided into four areas, or *suyu*s, for each of the four directions. The center was the capital, Cuzco, a holy city where only nobles were allowed to live. To the Incas, Cuzco was the center of the world.

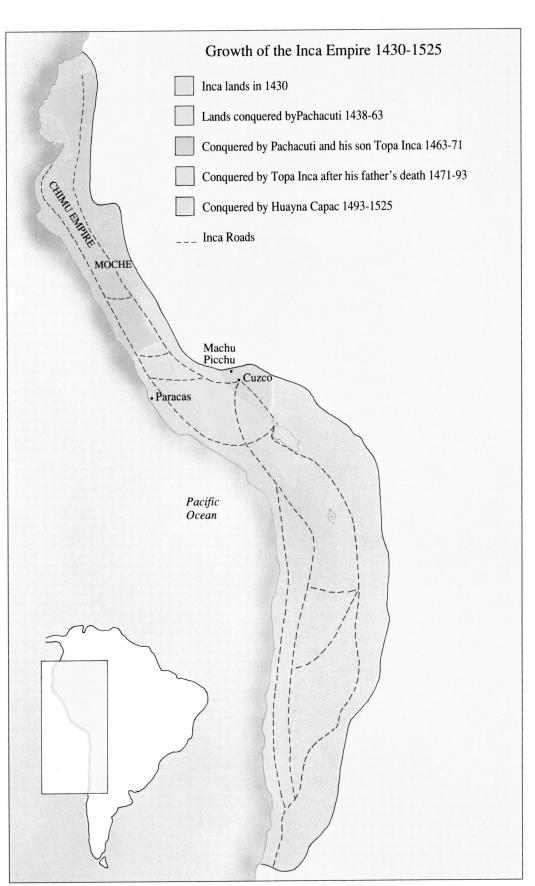

Growth of the Inca Empire 1430-1525

- Inca lands in 1430
- Lands conquered byPachacuti 1438-63
- Conquered by Pachacuti and his son Topa Inca 1463-71
- Conquered by Topa Inca after his father's death 1471-93
- Conquered by Huayna Capac 1493-1525
- - - - Inca Roads

CHIMU EMPIRE

MOCHE

Machu Picchu
• Cuzco
• Paracas

Pacific Ocean

BEFORE THE INCAS

Long before the time of the Incas, there were rich *civilizations* in and around the Andes. The Incas learned many things from these earlier peoples: how to weave cloth; how to build roads and bridges; and how to rule an empire. We know about the earlier peoples through objects – pottery, gold ornaments, and cloth found in their graves.

▲ This piece of cloth was worn by a *mummy* found at Paracas, on the southern coast of Peru. It is more than two thousand years old, yet, because of the dry desert air, it is perfectly preserved. We know little about the Paracas people, apart from their great skill at weaving and *embroidery*. They decorated their cloth with pictures of animals, using 190 different shades of colored thread.

Between A.D. 100 and 900, another ▶ civilization grew up around the Moche Valley on the northern coast. We know much more about the Moche (or Mochica) people, thanks to the fine pottery they buried with their dead. The pottery often shows scenes of ordinary life. The man on this pot is catching fish with a pelican. The pelican does the work but it is unable to swallow the fish because the man is holding it by the neck.

6

Warfare was very important to the Moche people. This statue is of a prisoner who has been captured in a battle. He has been stripped and tied to a wooden frame. His earlobe plugs, worn as a sign of high rank, have been taken – you can see the empty holes in his earlobes.

The Incas treated their prisoners of war just like this. No victory was complete until the defeated leaders had been *tortured* and killed. ▼

▲ Moche pottery is so skillfully made that it can show us what the people looked like. This is a portrait, probably of the person in whose tomb it was found.

◄ Some of the earlier people became powerful by conquering their neighbors, just as the Incas were to do. After A.D. 1000 a people called the Chimu conquered much of the north coast of Peru. The Chimu empire was well organized, with towns linked up by a network of roads and official messengers carrying news. The Chimu were also fine craftspeople, especially in gold. Look at this head of a puma, a wild cat. Notice its spiky whiskers.

Unlike the Incas, ► who lived high in the mountains, the Chimu were a coastal people. They fished from boats made of tightly bound reeds, like the one here made of pottery. In Peru today, people still sail reed boats much like this one.

Here is another ▶ piece of Chimu gold, a strange animal that might be a cat or a sea monster.

The Chimu empire was conquered by the Incas in the 1460s. The Incas were so impressed by the Chimu gold work that they took the best Chimu craftspeople back to their capital, Cuzco, to work for them.

To the Incas, gold was a holy metal. Their chief god was the sun, and they called gold "sweat of the sun." Silver was said to be "tears of the moon." This is a gold death mask, worn by a Chimu king or nobleman. ▼

9

THE SAPA INCA

The ruler of the empire was called the Sapa Inca, or "sole lord." He claimed to be a child of the sun and he was treated like a god. When a Sapa Inca died, his body was preserved and he continued to "live" in his palace. The dead Inca sat on a golden stool, watched over by a woman who whisked the flies from his face. The dead rulers were presented with food each day, and on special occasions they were all carried out of their palaces so that they could feast together. Each new ruler had to build himself a palace. By 1500 Cuzco was full of the palaces of dead Sapa Incas.

We know a lot about the lives of ▶ the Sapa Incas thanks to drawings made after the Incas had been conquered by the Spaniards in the 1530s. Pictures in this style were done by the artist Felipe Huaman Poma, the son of a Spanish conqueror and an Inca princess. This is his drawing of one of the last rulers, Manco Inca. He greets his chief nobles with a raised forefinger – the Inca salute. The nobles wear big earlobe plugs, which were signs of nobility. On his forehead, Manco has a red fringe, the Inca version of a crown. Manco and his men are getting ready for war.

10

The Sapa Inca and his Coya always traveled in a *litter*, sheltered under a covering of brightly colored feathers. Look at the strange headdresses of the men carrying the litter. The different peoples of the Inca Empire all had their own special headdresses. These men are Carabaya people. Compare their headdresses with those of the Lucana people carrying the litter on page 13. ▼

▲ This woman is a Coya, an Inca queen. Each Sapa Inca had many unofficial wives, and dozens of sons and daughters, who were the Inca nobility. Yet there was only one Coya, and she was always the ruler's own sister. Like him, she was thought to be a child of the sun. By marrying his sister, the Sapa Inca made sure that their children had only the pure blood of the sun. This was important because one of their sons would be the next Sapa Inca.

11

CONQUERING THE EMPIRE

The Incas were almost always successful in war, largely because of their great skill at organizing people and supplies. They could raise large armies and collect enough food to feed them for long periods. Using Inca roads, these armies were able to travel quickly. As the empire grew, the Incas were able to raise even bigger armies from the conquered lands. The only full-time soldiers were the Sapa Inca's bodyguard and his relatives, who were the captains and generals. Most of the fighters were farmers, who were called up when they were needed.

Inca soldiers were armed with short wooden clubs, tipped with stone or bronze – like the one held by this Moche warrior. They protected themselves with a wooden helmet and a small shield made from wood or deerskin.

The Sapa Inca often led his troops in person. This is Huayna Capac, going into battle carried on a litter. He is hurling a stone with a sling – a weapon always used at the start of battles. All the men were expert slingers. As children, they practiced by killing birds that came to feed on the crops.

◄ This is an Inca noble, dressed for war, painted on a wooden vase. His feathered helmet and spear are signs of his rank as an officer. Inca nobles were brought up to fight. They trained for warfare from the age of fourteen and were expected to prove their bravery and skill. Successful officers were rewarded with medals: silver badges that hung around their necks.

RULING THE EMPIRE

The Incas ruled over one of the best organized empires in history. They controlled the lives of everyone through a system of officials. This system was like a pyramid: at the bottom were millions of farmers; above them were thousands of officials and hundreds of higher officials; and above them were the four *governors* of the quarters of the empire. At the very top of the pyramid was the Sapa Inca.

People had to spend part of each year working for the state – mining, building roads, or serving in the army. Throughout the empire, there were great storehouses where food was kept. The Incas made sure that no one starved. In return, everyone was expected to work.

Although the Incas ▶ had no writing system, they could keep records using lengths of knotted string called *quipus*. The color of the string stood for whatever was being counted – for example, red string stood for warriors and yellow string stood for gold or corn. The knots stood for numbers. This is a quipu keeper, an official trained to understand the quipus. Quipus helped the Inca rulers to organize their empire – to raise armies and gather workers for building projects, and to collect enough food to feed them.

▲ You can see different sizes and types of knots on this quipu. A simple knot stands for one. Longer knots show numbers up to nine (like us, the Incas counted in tens). At the bottom of the string, the knots stand for units (ones). Higher up, they stand for tens, then hundreds, then thousands.

15

News was delivered very fast in the Inca empire by official messengers. They lived in huts placed every mile and a quarter along the roads. A messenger would run at great speed from his own hut to the next one, where another messenger would take the message on. With this system, important news could travel about 150 miles in one day. A messenger had to be a fast runner and have a good memory – messages had to be learned by heart as quickly as possible. This runner is blowing a note on a conch shell to let the next messenger know he is approaching. In his left hand, he holds a club and a sling for self-defense and a basket containing a quipu. He could be seen from a distance because he wore a headdress of white feathers.

There are many ▶ deep gorges and fast rivers in the Andes. Strong rope bridges were constructed across them. These bridges were regularly checked by officials and replaced when the rope became worn. The man on the left of this picture is an inspector of bridges. His headband and big earlobe plugs show that he is an Inca noble.

These are llamas, animals distantly related to camels. Like camels, llamas are useful because they can go without food or water for days. The Incas kept great herds of llamas to carry loads of food and other goods along the roads – to feed the armies and workers and to fill the storehouses. Llamas were also useful in providing wool, meat, and dung, which was burned as fuel. ▼

GODS

The Incas believed that a great god called Viracocha
made the world. Apart from Viracocha, who was
invisible, the Inca gods could be seen or felt. The most
important was Inti, the sun, who was believed to be the
father of the Sapa Inca and protector of the Inca people.
Like the Sapa Inca, he was married to his own sister,
Mama Quilla, the moon. Other gods included Pacha
Mama, the earth, and Illapa, thunder and lightning.

◄ This is an Inti Huatana, which means "post where the sun is tied." It was used to keep track of the sun's yearly movements. In the winter, for example, the sun sinks lower and lower in the sky. Eventually it reaches a point called a solstice, when it stops sinking and starts to rise again. The Incas knew when the solstice was due by looking at the shadow cast by this post. This was the signal for religious **ceremonies** to make the sun come back to warm the lands of the Incas. There were great celebrations when the sun started to rise again.

▲ As well as worshiping the great gods like Inti, the Incas worshiped *huacas*, which were holy or strange places or things. *Huacas* included rocks, springs, caves, mountains, rivers, and unusually shaped trees. All of these were thought to have special powers and the Incas made offerings to them to ask for their help. Less important *huacas* were offered corn beer. The more powerful *huacas* were offered **sacrifices**: children and llamas were killed and buried beside them. These important *huacas* had their own priests and priestesses who took care of them. This *huaca* is a holy spring at Tambo Machay, near Cuzco. The Incas channeled the water into the pool in the foreground.

19

coropo napampa saynam.

Throughout the year, there were many *festivals* in honor of the gods. Some were held to mark important events in the farming year, such as the harvesting of crops. Others marked big events in the lives of the people, such as the coming of age of the young Incas. During the festivals, people feasted, drank beer, and danced. Here, the women are singing and beating on drums. The men, dressed as birds, are getting ready to dance.

FARMING

The mountains of the Andes are not easy places to grow food. *Droughts*, poor soil, bad frosts, and steep slopes all make farming difficult. The Incas found solutions to all these problems, thanks to ingenious techniques and their great skill at organizing people.

◀ The problem of steep slopes and poor soil was solved by building flat raised strips called terraces. These were made by building long stone walls and then piling up soil from the valleys behind them. The soil was made *fertile* with seabird droppings. These terraces, at Pisac, were planned by professional Inca *architects*.

Lack of water was solved by building stone ▶ *reservoirs* to store the rain until it was needed. The Incas also made stone-lined *irrigation* channels, carrying water from rivers and mountain streams to the tops of the terraces. It was then channeled down the hillside through the crops. In the cold, higher terraces the Incas grew potatoes, which can withstand frost. Farther down they grew corn. This woman is opening an irrigation channel to water the growing corn plants.

21

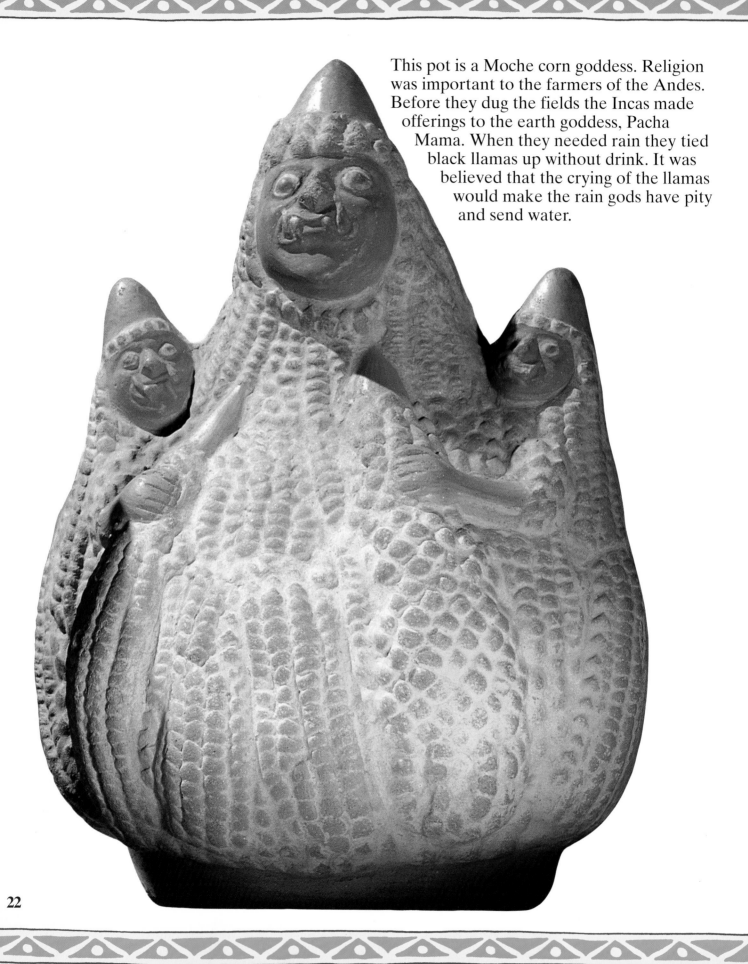

This pot is a Moche corn goddess. Religion was important to the farmers of the Andes. Before they dug the fields the Incas made offerings to the earth goddess, Pacha Mama. When they needed rain they tied black llamas up without drink. It was believed that the crying of the llamas would make the rain gods have pity and send water.

◀ This piece of wood, carved and painted like the head of a puma, is a drinking cup. It would have been used to drink beer made from corn. Everyone from the Sapa Inca down to the poorest farmer drank this beer, called *chicha*. It was made by old women who chewed the grains of corn and then spat them into jars of warm water. This process made the corn break down, producing alcohol. Eight days later it was ready for drinking.

Men and women worked together in the ▶ fields. The men dug into the soil with long wooden foot plows, called *tacclas*. The women crouched in front of them, breaking up the earth with their hands. This drawing (by Felipe Huaman Poma) shows the Sapa Inca himself (far left) digging, watched over by his father, the sun god. On the right his Coya brings him a golden cup filled with corn beer, so that he can drink a toast to the sun. This was a religious ceremony to ensure a good harvest. The men and women sing as they work.

BUILDING

The Incas were wonderful builders with stone. Using only bronze chisels and stone hammers, they cut enormous blocks into different shapes and sizes, fitting them together like pieces in a jigsaw puzzle. This method made Inca walls much stronger than any built today. In 1950 two-thirds of Cuzco was wrecked in a terrible earthquake. But not one of the old Inca walls collapsed.

It was said to have taken seventy-five years to build this fortress, Sacsahuaman, overlooking Cuzco. Twenty thousand men worked on it. Four thousand of them worked in the *quarries*, cutting the stones. Six thousand men dragged the stones on wooden rollers to the site. Here, ten thousand men were kept busy, building earth ramps to raise the blocks, dragging the blocks up the ramps, and then shaping them and fitting them into place. Some of these stones are over 20 feet high and weigh more than 100 tons.

A doorway from ▶
the same fortress
gives a closer view of
the stone blocks.
They fit so tightly that
it is impossible to slip
a knife blade between
them. Inca doorways
and windows were
always wide at the
bottom and narrow at
the top. This made
them strong.

This aerial view of
Machu Picchu shows
the size of Inca
building projects. On
the right are the
houses and temples.
On the left are the
great terraces for
farming. Machu
Picchu is the most
famous Inca site
because it is so well
preserved. It was
abandoned by the
Incas for some
unknown reason and
only rediscovered
in 1911. ▼

WEAVING

It was the women who made the Inca clothes, using cotton and wool – especially the fine wool of the alpaca, a smaller relative of the llama. Llama wool, which was coarser, was used for blankets. The first stage was coloring the wool, using dyes from plants and shellfish. Then it was spun by hand into fine thread. Finally, it was woven into pieces of cloth on a loom.

◄ This woman is weaving cloth using a backstrap loom. One end is strapped around her back while the other end is tied to a tree. She passes the colored thread from side to side, weaving it in between the lengthwise threads. In South America today, women still weave cloth this way.

Some Inca tunics ► have survived, showing what skilled weavers the women were. Look at the complicated patterns in the small boxes and the flowers and animals on the white tunic. You can see a tunic just like this in the drawing by Felipe Huaman Poma on page 23.

This hat, worn by ▶
an Inca noble, has
been carefully woven
and then decorated
with feathers.
Compare it with the
hat worn by the noble
in the painting on
page 29.

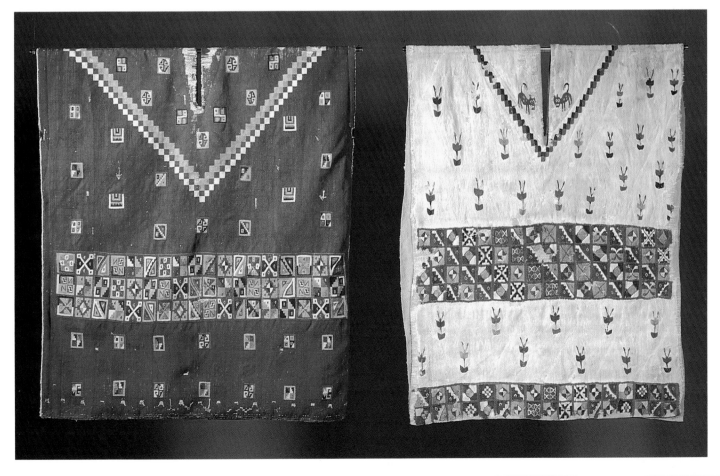

THE FALL OF THE INCAS

The Inca Empire fell apart in a very short time, soon after the death of the great ruler Huayna Capac in 1525. Two of his sons – Atahuallpa and Huascar – argued over which of them should be the next Sapa Inca. They fought a bloody war against each other, which ended in Atahuallpa's victory in 1532. While the war was still going on news came that strange people had arrived on the coast. Everything about these visitors seemed odd – they dressed in metal suits, rode on unknown animals (horses), and had hair growing out of their chins. They were Spaniards, warlike people who had recently arrived in the Americas. Atahuallpa had heard about these people from his father, and, after his victory, he invited them to visit him. There were fewer than two hundred of them, so he felt no reason to be afraid of them.

This picture by ▶ Theodore de Bry, though inaccurate in its details (the Incas would have been clothed), shows what happened next. Without warning, the Spaniards fired their cannon and charged at the Inca's army. Cutting down all the warriors who tried to protect Atahuallpa, the Spaniards took him prisoner. The Spaniards promised to free Atahuallpa in exchange for a huge ransom in gold. The Incas paid the ransom, but instead of freeing Atahuallpa, the Spaniards killed him.

This painted ▶
wooden jar shows
an Inca view of the
Spaniards and the
Africans they brought
with them. An Inca
noble walks behind a
Spanish trumpeter
and an African
drummer.

Spanish rule
brought many
changes to life in the
Andes. The Inca
religion was stamped
out and people were
forced to become
Christians. The
Spaniards did not
understand the Inca
farming system and
the irrigation canals
were left to crumble.
Millions of people
died from diseases,
like smallpox, brought
from Europe.

◀ Despite the
destruction of the
Inca empire, many
things about ordinary
life have not changed
in the Andes. Today,
people still spin and
weave wool in the old
way. They still use
llamas to carry their
goods. They still dress
up in colorful
costumes and dance
to celebrate festivals.   **29**

GLOSSARY

Architects People who design buildings and other things, such as parks.

Ceremonies Formal acts, such as religious celebrations.

Christians People who believe in the divinity of Jesus Christ and in his teachings.

Civilization A particular group of people and the way that they live.

Conquests Lands taken over after battle.

Droughts Long periods without rain.

Embroidery Decorative needlework that makes a picture or a pattern.

Empire A large area of land, including its different peoples, ruled by a single state.

Fertile Able to create new life. Fertile fields are those which are good for the growing of plants.

Festival A celebration, like a big party, to mark an important event.

Governors People who rule areas of a country.

Irrigation The system of storing and directing water for farming.

Litter A chair carried on poles. The Sapa Inca and his family rode on litters. Everyone else had to walk – the Incas had no animals big enough to ride and they knew nothing about the wheel.

Mummy A preserved dead body. Dead Sapa Incas were made into mummies, which were then treated with all the honors given to the living ruler. Other nobles were also made into mummies.

Quarries Open mines where stones are cut or dug up.

Quipus Lengths of knotted string used to record information. Quipus were said to be used by the Incas to record their history, but no one knows how this was done.

Reservoir An artificial pool or container made for storing large amounts of water.

Sacrifices People or animals killed as offerings to a god or goddess.

Tortured Made to suffer extreme pain.

IMPORTANT DATES

400 B.C. – Paracas people, on the southern coast of Peru, make fine weaving
A.D. 100-900 – The Moche civilization grows on the northern coast of Peru
1000-1460s – Chimu people conquer an empire on the northern coast of Peru
1200-1300 – The Incas settle in the Cuzco valley
1438-63 – Pachacuti Inca conquers the people to the west of Cuzco
1463-71 – Pachacuti and his son Topa Inca conquer the Chimu empire

1471-93 – Topa Inca conquers the southern part of the empire, now part of Chile
1492 – Spanish ships, captained by Columbus, first reach the Americas
1493-1525 – Huayna Capac conquers more lands in the north
1525-32 – War between Huayna Capac's sons, Atahuallpa and Huascar
1532 – Spaniards, led by Francisco Pizarro, capture Atahuallpa
1536 – Manco Inca leads an unsuccessful uprising against the Spaniards

PRONUNCIATION

Many of the Inca names look difficult to pronounce. It helps if you remember that "Hua" sounds like "wa" and "qui" sounds like "kee." So "quipu" sounds like "kee-poo," "huaca" is "waka," and "Tahuantisuyu" is "Ta-wan-tee-soo-yoo."

BOOKS TO READ

Baquedano, Elizabeth. *Aztec, Inca and Maya.* Eyewitness Books. New York: Alfred A. Knopf Books for Young Readers, 1993.

Chrisp, Peter. *Spanish Conquests in the New World.* Exploration and Encounters. New York: Thomson Learning, 1993.

Kuss, Daniele. *The Incas.* North Bellmore, NY: Marshall Cavendish, 1991.

Marrin, Albert. *Inca and Spaniard: Pizarro and the Conquest of Peru.* New York: Macmillan Children's Book Group, 1989.

Morrison, Marion. *Ecuador, Peru, and Bolivia.* World in View. Milwaukee: Raintree Steck-Vaughn, 1992.

Newman, Shirlee P. *The Incas.* First Books. New York: Franklin Watts, 1992.

INDEX